This book belongs to

Dana Wunderlich

The Clumsiest Cowboy

A Lesson in Showing Compassion

by
Doug Peterson

Illustrated by
Paul Conrad

SCHOLASTIC INC.

New York Toronto London Auckland Sydney
Mexico City New Delhi Hong Kong Buenos Aires

Cowboy Larry slowly moved toward the snorting bull. "Easy, boy, easy," he said to the bull. "Take a deep breath."

A group of cowboys sat on the fence, watching the master at work. Larry was known far and wide as the Compassionate Cowboy. He drifted from town to town, helping animals with their problems.

Cowboy Larry had faced it all. He had helped pigs that didn't like being dirty, chickens that bickered, and prairie dogs with family problems. He had even written a book called *Cows That Stampede and the People Who Love Them.*

Today, he was helping a bull control his anger.

"Get in touch with your feelings," said Cowboy Larry, taking a step closer to the dangerous bull. "Just say to yourself—"

"Whoaaaaa!"

Larry tripped on a dodge ball. He tumbled into a water barrel, which toppled onto its side and rolled downhill.

WHAM!

The barrel shattered against the fence, sending Larry soaring.

"YOWWWW!"

He crash-landed on his wooden horse
and got two nasty splinters.

Leaping from his horse, Larry bounced off the top of a covered wagon as if he were on a trampoline.

Then he crashed on the ground, smashing his cowboy hat down over his eyes.

Larry wasn't just a compassionate cowboy. He was also the clumsiest cowpoke in the west.

SMACK!

Larry tried and tried to pull his cowboy hat off his eyes, but it was no use.

His hat was jammed onto his head tighter than a rattlesnake in a root beer bottle.

Meanwhile, the cowboys couldn't stop laughing at Cowboy Larry's clumsiness.

Even the bull rolled on the ground, snorting with laughter.

"Hey, you done cured my bull," one cowboy said. "He's not angry anymore!"

"You're amazing, Larry," said another cowboy, still giggling.

Cowboy Larry had helped the bull get over his anger, but Cowboy Larry still felt bad about his clumsiness. Whenever he tripped and fell, which he did a lot, no one seemed to care.

Everyone just laughed.

No one helped poor Larry yank his hat off his head. So he just bumbled around Dodge Ball City, unable to see where he was going.

Cowboy Larry was supposed to lead a support group for shy roosters later that afternoon. But because he couldn't see, Cowboy Larry spent the entire time talking to bales of hay.

No one helped him. No one had compassion. They thought it was a hoot watching Cowboy Larry stumble around.

Next, Cowboy Larry went to the I'm OK, You're OK Corral. He was supposed to help a group of cows find their "personal space" in the pasture. But because Larry couldn't see, he spent the entire time talking to tumbleweeds.

OWN YOUR OWN SPACE!

THE GRASS IS GREENER ON YOUR SIDE OF THE FENCE!

No one did a thing to help. Everyone laughed and laughed until tears came to their eyes.

Finally, Larry decided to go to the Clip-Clop Horseshoe Store. There, he used a shoehorn to pry the hat off his eyes. But just as he got his hat off, he stumbled backward into a shelf, knocking down several boxes of horseshoes.

When the heavy horseshoes hit a loose floorboard, Larry flew straight up into the ceiling. His hat jammed down over his eyes once again. This time the hat was stuck on his head snugger than a bull in tights.

Still no one cared.

"No one cares a stitch that I can't see where I'm going," Larry muttered to himself sadly. "So I'm gonna mosey out of town to see if they even care that I'm gone."

But no one cared. In fact, people didn't even notice that Larry had left. They were too excited about the Stuff-Mart Wagon, which had just rolled into town. The wagon had a load of brand-new Cactus Patch Dolls.

So poor Cowboy Larry left town all alone, riding backwards on

a very confused cow, which Cowboy Larry thought was his horse.

"I'm glad that at least God cares about me," Larry muttered to the cow.

"At least God knows that—"

Suddenly Cowboy Larry heard a very strange sound coming from the town.

"OW! OH! OW! OH!"

Someone was hurt.

Larry wanted to just keep on riding. But he knew what it was like to be hurt. He cared. So Larry turned the cow around and galloped back into town.

"What seems to be the problem?" asked
Larry, who still couldn't see because of his hat.

"It's the new dolls!" shouted Junior Asparagus.
"The Cactus Patch Dolls are made
with real cactus needles!"

"You mean—"

"Yes!" Junior exclaimed. "We all have cactus needles sticking us
like . . . like we're pin cushions."

"I feel your pain," said Larry. "Say, if you help me get this hat off my head so that I can see, I'll be happy to help the whole town remove all those cactus needles."

So Junior Asparagus helped pull the hat off Larry's head. Then Larry the Compassionate Cowboy spent the rest of the day helping all the townsfolk remove their cactus needles.

The townsfolk suddenly realized that Cowboy Larry saw things more clearly than they did. All day long Cowboy Larry had seen their troubles. But they hadn't seen that Cowboy Larry also needed help. He needed comfort whenever he tripped and fell.

Finally, their eyes were open. It was like someone had taken hats off their eyes, too.

"We're sorry we never helped you before," said an old cowpoke.

"From now on, we'll care," said another. "We'll be compassionate cowboys too."

"That's great news!" said Cowboy Larry, as he moseyed toward his wooden horse. "Say! What's this?"

The people of the town had put a brand-new saddle on Cowboy Larry's horse. That way, maybe he wouldn't get so many splinters.

They truly cared.

Everyone gathered on the edge of town to say farewell

as the Compassionate Cowboy rode off into the sunset.

"Adios, amigos!" Cowboy Larry shouted. "Happy trails to—"

CLUNK!

Cowboy Larry's horse hit a pothole, and the Compassionate Cowboy
tumbled headfirst onto the ground. He landed on his ten-gallon hat.
But this time, *everybody* helped him get back up.

. . . All comfort comes from Him [God]. He comforts us in all our troubles.
Now we can comfort others when they are in trouble . . .
2 Corinthians 1:3–4